THE PERFECT ORANGE

Rayve Productions Inc.
Box 726 Windsor CA 95492 USA

Text copyright © 1994 Frank P. Araujo
Illustrations copyright © 1994 Xiao Jun Li

Print production coordinator: Kim McDonell
Printed in Hong Kong through Pan Pacific Graphics, San Ramon

Publisher's Cataloging in Publication
  Araujo, Frank P.
  The perfect orange: a tale from Ethiopia /
  by Frank P. Araujo; illustrated by Xiao Jun Li.
  p. cm. -- (Toucan tales)
  ISBN 1-877810-94-0
  SUMMARY: Retelling of an Ethiopian folktale about a generous
     and caring little girl of long ago.
  1. Tales--Ethiopia--Juvenile literature. 2. Folklore--Ethiopia--Juvenile literature.
  3. Folklore--Ethiopia.   I. Li, Xiao Jun, ill. II. Title. III. Series.

  GR356.A73 1994   398.2'0963

Library of Congress Catalog Card Number 94-67524

Toucan Tales series

  Volume 1   *NEKANE, THE LAMIÑA & THE BEAR*
                 A Tale of the Basque Pyrenees

  Volume 2   *THE PERFECT ORANGE*
                 A Tale from Ethiopia

THE PERFECT ORANGE

A Tale from Ethiopia

Frank P. Araujo, PhD

illustrations by Xiao Jun Li

Once, in the mountains of Ethiopia lived an orphan girl named Tshai [tsuh-HIGH]. Because she was sincere and generous, her neighbors loved her dearly.

One morning Tshai went out into the orchard
by her hut. She saw a big, bright orange.

"A perfect orange!" she cried. "I must take it
to our ruler, the great *Nigus* [NI-goose]."

Tshai plucked the orange, put on her whitest
shamma, and started for the city.

On her way, Tshai passed by the great house of *Ato Jib*, the Lord Hyena.

"Where are you going, little girl?" called out Ato Jib.

"To the city with a perfect orange," she replied.

"Give me the orange and I will give you a gourd to carry water," said Ato Jib leering.

"No," said Tshai. "I am taking this orange to the great Nigus."

Ato Jib laughed so hard, he rolled on the ground.

"What a silly gift," he said. "You must take
the Nigus something precious, like a gold cross or
a rare jewel."

Tshai ignored his laughter and went on her way.

In the city, Tshai found the royal palace.

"I'd like to see the great Nigus," she said to the *Agafari*, the Royal Chamberlain.

The Agafari scowled from behind his handsome moustache.

"His Majesty is very busy," he snapped.

"I only need a moment to give His Majesty this orange," replied Tshai with her biggest smile.

The Agafari's face softened.

"Very well," he said and he showed Tshai into the throne room.

"Welcome," said the Nigus. "How may we serve you?"

Tshai gave a curtsy and said, "When I saw this perfect orange, I thought it would be just the right gift for your Majesty."

The Nigus accepted the orange with a smile. "It is a perfect orange, My daughter. We thank you greatly. Now, what do you wish in return?"

"Nothing, Your Majesty," Tshai said with a little smile..

"But you have pleased Us, My daughter," said the Nigus. "Take this purse of gold."

"No, thank you, Your Majesty," replied Tshai.

"Then have this casket of jewels," he said.

"I need nothing," said Tshai. She bowed and left the room.

When Tshai left, the Nigus called his Agafari. "The little girl refused Our gifts," he said. "Go and choose one of Our finest donkeys. Put this purse of gold and this casket of jewels in the saddle bags. Then follow and give her the donkey."

The Agafari ran with the donkey until he was out of breath. Finally, he caught up with Tshai.

"Little girl," he said, "His Majesty wants you to have this donkey."

"For me?" she said clapping her hands. "Please thank His Majesty."

The Agafari lifted Tshai onto the donkey's back and waved good-bye.

When Tshai passed the house of Ato Jib, the hyena's mouth popped open.

"Where did you get the donkey?" he asked.

"His Majesty gave it to me," Tshai said, and she continued on her way.

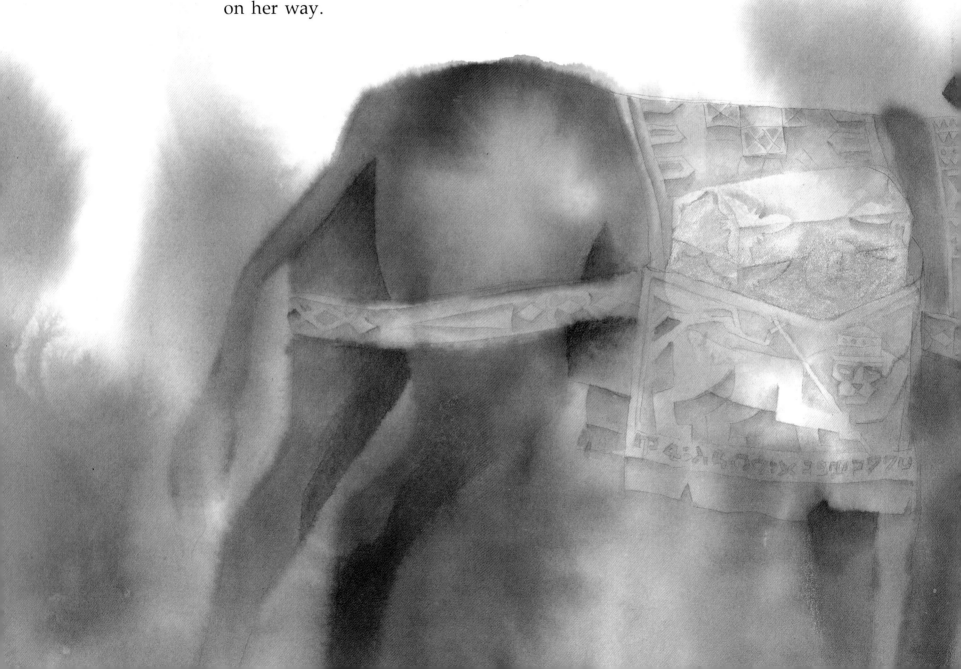

Ato Jib's eyes narrowed.

"A donkey with full saddle bags for an orange!" he muttered.

"What would the Nigus give me for my cattle and lands?"

Dashing off, the hyena wrote out a deed for his lands and his cattle. Then, he put on his fanciest *shamma* and set out for the city.

Ato Jib arrived at the palace. "I am an important fellow," he said to the Agafari. "I have cattle and lands to give the great Nigus."

The Agafari frowned and stroked his great moustache. But then he smiled, nodded his head, and let Ato Jib in.

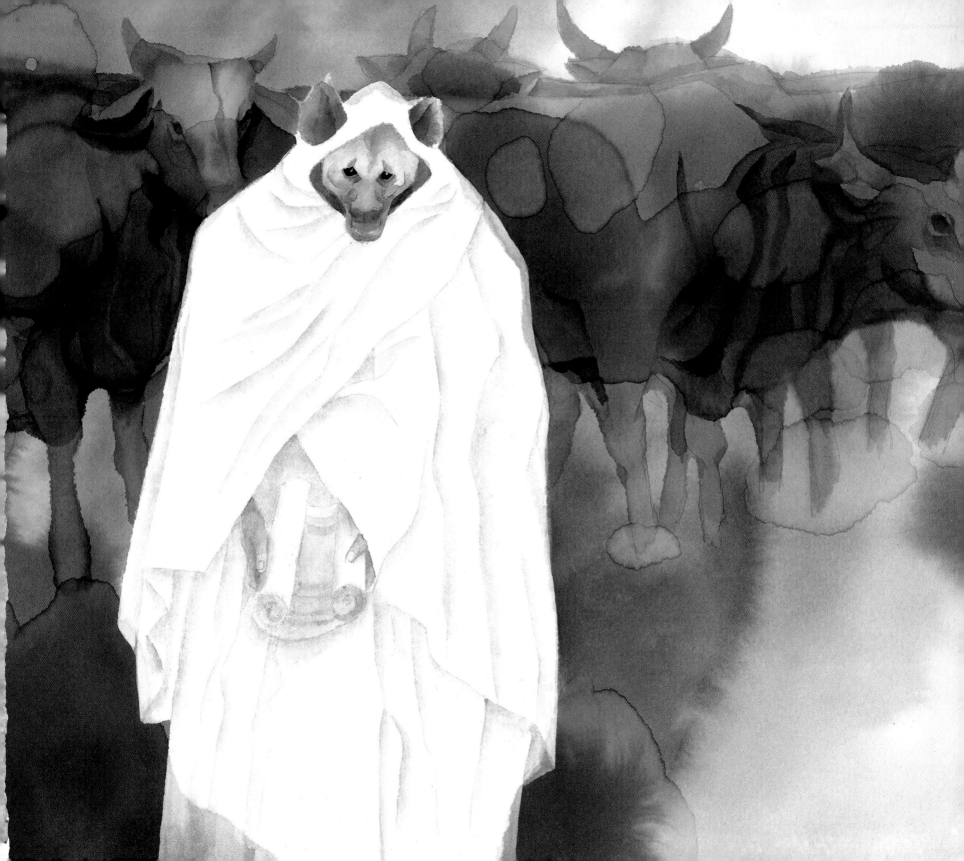

Ato Jib's black nose brushed the toe of his sandal as he bowed before the Nigus. "Your Majesty," he said waving the deed, "I am pleased to give you all my lands and cattle."

"These are great gifts, Ato Jib," said the Nigus. "What may We give you in return?"

The hyena drooled and bowed again, this time banging his head on the carpet.

"Whatever Your Majesty deems worthy for my humble offerings," he replied.

The Nigus smiled.

"We will bestow on you Our most prized possession.

Here, good fellow, We give you this perfect orange."

When Tshai reached her village, her neighbors ran out to admire her donkey.

One of them looked in the saddle bags. "Look," she cried, "His Majesty gave you gold and jewels."

"What a surprise!" cried Tshai. "Friends, please help me celebrate this good fortune."

They prepared a great feast of *anjira*, *wat*, and *zighni*. After dinner, Tshai played a song on her *krar*, and they all ate oranges for dessert.

AUTHOR'S NOTES

I collected this story while working on an economic development program in the Harare region of Ethiopia and have found different versions of this same tale in Eritrea and Somalia. The Ethiopian version is my favorite.

The Amharic words and names used in this story are given below with their meanings and a pronunciation guide. For my part, I would like to express my appreciation to those Ethiopian friends who shared the original story with me. I will always remember with great pleasure working with the wonderful Ethiopian people in their beautiful country.

—F.A.

A GLOSSARY OF ETHIOPIAN TERMS

agafari [ah-ga-FAH-ree]:   chamberlain, attendant

anjira [an-JI-rah]:   Ethiopian (pancake-like) bread

ato [AH-toe]:   lord, mister

jib [jib]:   hyena

krar [krahr]:   harp

nigus [NI-goose]:   king

shamma [SHAWM-mah]:   white gown

tshai [tsuh-HIGH]:   sun

wat [wahtt]:   spicy sauce

zighni [ZIG-nee]:   spicy Ethiopian curry